I hope
the si...

Bette

Home At Last

TRUE LOST DOG STORIES

Bette Anunson Anderson

PAGE PUBLISHING, INC.
Conneaut Lake, PA

First originally published by Page Publishing 2019

Cover image courtesy of RB

ISBN 978-1-64584-002-2 (pbk)
ISBN 978-1-64584-003-9 (digital)

Printed in the United States of America

Dedicated to…
Many of us have angels in disguise slipping in and out of our
lives giving us support and guidance when we need it most.
I've had more than my share of angels. The
animals and I will be eternally grateful.
This book is dedicated to my angels.
Bette

Shadow

The minute George and Judy stepped outside, the driving and swirling snow stung their faces, and the piercing cold snapped at their cheeks and nostrils.

They both spotted the empty doghouse at the same time.

"No! It can't be!" Judy screamed, but it was—Shadow was gone!

"My heart stopped," Judy would tell me later. She continued, "It was hard to breathe, let alone think. We had just heard the weather report—twenty degrees below zero and a wind-chill factor of fifty degrees below zero. How had Shadow slipped his collar? How far could a blind dog go?" An ad in the local newspaper had grabbed my attention. "Lost—blind collie—$100 reward." Little did George and Judy know then that this night would be the beginning of one of the most painful periods in their lives. It was a beginning in many ways. It was the start of a difficult search for their beloved dog, and it was a beginning for me—the start of my Lost Dog Project.

My conversation that night with Judy, the owner, challenged me. I sensed Judy was in tears as we hung up the phone. She probably didn't realize that I, a complete stranger, was in tears too.

Over the years, especially in winter, I have thought of that time in my life and the missing dog named Shadow. He was handsome and sweet, a gentle spirit who took whatever life handed him and made the most of it.

Shadow loved the cold weather, and with his silky blond fur blowing in the wind, he seemed to glide across the snow. He ran smooth and steady, not jerky, with high steps as most blind dogs do. You just knew he was a dog filled with confidence and joy.

But life had not started out joyful for Shadow. It took love—lots of love.

A country home in northeastern Wisconsin was to be Shadow's home. Summers can be warm, but winters are mostly cold, so cold in fact that the huge bay of Green Bay sometimes freezes over.

The whole area is best known as the home of the Green Bay Packers; but to the people in the area, it's known as a family town, and most people include their pets as part of the family. Shadow was destined to be one of those dogs.

Our story of Shadow starts out one cold January day.

A pretty, fluffy, blond-and-white collie appeared at the door of George and Judy Fuller's house. It was quickly apparent that the dog was blind or almost blind. Even though the Fullers were new to Little Suamico, a little community close to Green Bay, it didn't take long for them to find out the dog belonged to a neighbor.

When George came knocking at their door, the neighbors said, "Not much good for anything. If you want him, you can keep him." Not too happy with the caustic remark and always ready to help an animal in trouble, the Fullers took him home.

The next week included a visit to a renowned animal eye specialist, Dr. Sam Vainisi, who had retired to the Green Bay area. "It's a congenital condition. Nothing can be done. He will only see shadows for the rest of his life."

Discouraged, George and Judy discussed the options for the dog on the way home. Judy remembered thinking about him that day. He was sweet but reserved and shy; but now that he was confirmed blind, would he ever find a home if they took him to an animal shelter?

On one of my first meetings with Judy, she related her frustrations about her love for dogs. "Why me? Doesn't anybody else care? One more mouth to feed, one more doghouse to clean, and one more dog for vaccinations. By the time we got home, the decision had been made. We had one more dog, and the name came easily. Shadow seemed appropriate."

Shadow fit the family like a glove. He was now just one of the pack. Most days included a long walk in the woods behind the house where Shadow mingled well with all the other dogs. He especially liked a dog named Whiskey, a vivacious yellow Lab. Whiskey needed a companion as much as Shadow did, a friend to bounce and play with and to use up the unstoppable energy.

Thinking of ways to make Shadow's life better, Judy decided to put a bell on Whiskey. Now they could always be together. When you saw Shadow, you saw Whiskey nearby.

Wide-open spaces, not barbed-wire fences, were meant for Shadow. Judy's story of one of Shadow's escapades was fascinating.

"I cringed the first time I saw Shadow bolt toward a fence that was right at his eye level. He hit the fence hard, bounced back, and fell to the ground. Whiskey looked at me and then back to Shadow. Less than fifteen minutes later, Shadow raced to the fence again. George instinctively yelled, 'Fence!' Shadow slowed and then hit the fence again! But we both noticed he had hesitated for just a moment. We wondered, *did it mean something?* We purposely stayed out in the yard and waited to see if he would do it again. Then it happened! As he headed for the fence, George shouted, 'Fence!' Shadow dropped to the ground and crawled under the fence. We looked at each other, stunned. We knew right then this was one special dog."

Winter was coming, and with it came the nights. Judy lay awake worrying about other people's animals. Were their shelters good enough? Worse yet, did they even have a shelter? At their house, three of the big dogs stayed outside but had insulated doghouses filled with straw. Several years later, the Fullers would add a large fenced area around the doghouses; but for now, the doghouses would have to do. Vet bills and dog food already drained their limited budget.

It was February, and Little Suamico was well into a long cold spell. George and Judy went outside to do their customary check of the dogs before going to bed.

Gone! Shadow was gone! How? Why? But the bottom line was, it didn't matter. Nothing else really mattered except that Shadow was gone, and they *had* to find him.

"Gusts of wind hit our faces as we checked out our yard and outbuildings," Judy explained. "Snow had already blanketed any tracks. Next, we searched all the neighbors' yards and outbuildings, crunching through the snow step by step. No Shadow!"

"We climbed into the Jeep and headed out into the storm. George tried to stay on the road and see where he was going while I held the flashlight, stopping every so often to get a better look at something. Gusts of wind blew snow across the road, swirling even worse when trucks passed." Driving slow did nothing to endear us to anyone behind us. I could just imagine their angry thoughts: *Get off the road!*

"As we drove, worrisome thoughts of Shadow kept going through my head," Judy continued. "Would we find him in the spring? That beautiful blond fur sticking grotesquely out of a snow bank, a victim of those menacing snowplows?"

"Traffic got lighter as it neared one o'clock in the morning. Then two o'clock. Still no Shadow. We headed home at three o'clock, hoping to get some sleep so we could go out again early in the morning.

"Exhausted but unable to sleep and knowing most of the people in the area were farmers and would be up early, we dragged ourselves out of bed by seven o'clock. Not hungry, a condition that persisted all the time Shadow was gone, we headed out again to knock on doors until ten o'clock. Once back home, we started calling everyone we could think of—the sheriff's department, the animal shelters, the local dog catcher, and the man supervising the county plows."

They stopped bus drivers and postal carriers, begging them to watch for their beloved Shadow. A local snowmobile club volunteered in the search. Rick, the Fullers' son, spent all his waking hours searching, except for when he was at school.

The ad in the local paper that read, "One-hundred-dollar reward—blind collie—blond and white," grabbed my attention. As a faithful reader of the lost-and-found ads, I was always trying to match up the ads with the found animals at the Humane Society in Green Bay. The shelter was an organization that I had helped organize in 1958.

Being in real estate allowed me to be flexible with my time, and I made the most of it in the next two weeks. I spent hours and hours riding around looking for Shadow, sometimes with Judy, sometimes alone. Day after day we looked, still nothing. We couldn't give up.

There were no phone calls or sightings of a dog like Shadow, only calls with the question, "Did you find him?" People really cared. Most conversations ended with, "Would you please let us know?"

And then I began to think, "Why am I driven to find Shadow?" I had never even seen him. Could it be because I had lost one of our dogs several years before? Dear old Ginger, deaf at fourteen years old, had wandered away late one night in March when I took one of the other dogs back in the house. Sheer terror had engulfed me. I had wondered, *would she drown in the river that ran in front of the house?* It had been open in areas with water and chunks of ice rushing past, or would she get hit by a car at the busy road in back of the house? Neither happened. I still remember the feeling of panic even though she had been gone only a few hours. Fortunately, our friend Jake found her sitting on someone's porch, trying to get in.

George even hired a plane to fly over the frozen bay, which was only a mile from the Fullers' home. The pilot charged him only five dollars for gas. What a break for someone who lived paycheck to paycheck. Neither one of them spotted a dog.

The second week Shadow was missing, George was on a coffee break with the guys at work. One of the guys mentioned that he had seen a blind dog when he was ice fishing on the east side of the bay. Could it be? Then George thought, "No, he said, 'east side,'" but the area he described was directly across the bay from Little Suamico and George and Judy's house! The guy admitted he gave the dog a sandwich and now was wondering what happened to the dog! George's mind raced as angry thoughts ran through his head.

"What do you think would happen to the dog, you dummy? Especially a blind one," but he held his temper and quizzed the guy. "Did he act okay? Could he walk all right?" It crossed my mind that Judy would not have been so nice.

Over the years, I came to know the real Judy. She had a heart of gold for animals and was driven to care about any animal she thought needed help. Her world revolved around her family, her home, and her animals. Even with so many animals in the house, it was spotless. Her floors were scrubbed daily, and her yard was always kept up with pretty flowers. Fortunately, George loved the animals every bit as much. It was obvious that their pets were a financial burden and required George to work two jobs and Judy to do part-time work just to keep up.

What do we do now? I had wondered. Years later, I would discover that one of the best ways to locate lost animals was to put up real estate signs or cover old political yard signs with just three or four lines that you can read driving by at fifty-five or sixty miles an hour, but I hadn't thought of that yet.

George and Judy had run a radio ad on Shadow, shortly after he was lost but decided to run the ad on the radio again. This time, saying the dog might be on the east side of the bay. A call came in almost at once. Sadly, no one was home. The message on the voice mail said, "Hey, I saw a blind dog, and I live near Champion which is only three or four miles from the bay." The caller didn't leave his phone number, and there was no caller ID at that time. Our hearts sank. We plummeted to the bottom of what felt like a roller coaster ride.

If Shadow had really traveled that far, he would have fought the drifting snow all the way to the bay, then crossed ten to fifteen miles of its windswept ice, then another three or four miles climbing the very steep and rocky hills at the water's edge and on through the heavily wooded areas, and then the frozen, plowed fields to Champion. Could it really be him? Was someone playing a cruel trick?

Struggling to remain positive after two weeks of frigid weather, we felt our hearts race as we talked and planned. What do we do next? What if we went through all this only to be a day or two or even hours too late? There was only one answer. We had to find the man who saw the dog.

Luckily, at that time, the Green Bay phone directory had separate listings for the city and the outlying communities such as Champion. Another plus, Champion was just a dot on the map, so there shouldn't be many phone numbers.

Judy started calling at the beginning of the Champion phone numbers, and I started at the end. Within minutes, I was talking to the man who had left the message. I took his number and had him call Judy. His description of Shadow was perfect, and he said he remembered the area where he saw the dog. She reminded him of the hundred-dollar reward, which was a big motivation for him and his wife to begin their search.

Within two hours, he called back. They saw the dog. The dog had made a weak attempt to get into the woods, but they had caught him. What a relief.

George and Judy were on their way in minutes, but first, they had to stop at Judy's mom's house to borrow some of the reward money. Luckily for them, she was an animal lover too!

When they drove up to the house in Champion, Judy could not force herself to go inside the home with George, so she stayed inside the car. What if it wasn't Shadow? The wait was agonizing.

George entered the home and approached the dog lying on the floor. The dog's heavy breathing gave a hint of the pneumonia that had engulfed him. His eyes were cloudy. His feet were raw and bloody, yet Shadow's reaction when he sniffed at George's hands was enough to tell George that Shadow knew he was safe at last. The loss of twenty-five pounds had him looking like a ghost of the former beauty he had been.

Picking up the dog, George came out of the house and slowly walked down the steps toward his car. All Judy could see was matted fur, a limp, straggly tail, and what appeared to be blood on the dog's feet. Her heart sank. This dog looked way too small to be Shadow, but then, George opened the car door and put the bundle of fur on Judy's lap. Those blind but beautiful brown eyes gave him away. Shadow nuzzled in her neck as tears streamed down Judy's face. It was Shadow, and he was finally going home!

George, Judy, and Shadow (and Whiskey too) would make sure they were never more than a few feet apart for the rest of their lives.

Shadow and Judy

Judy Fuller of Little Suamico holds the family collie, Shadow, after it was found. The dog is blind and wandered away from home in February.

Lassie's rival

Blind collie is home again

By JULIE SCHAEFER
Of the Press-Gazette

When it comes to poignant dog stories, Shadow can out-finesse even Lassie.

Shadow is the 2-year-old blind collie who took off on a winter odyssey. It eventually cost his owners, George and Judy Fuller of Little Suamico, much time, money and heartache, and it nearly cost Shadow his life.

The yarn begins on Feb. 10, the frigid and windy eve of our last big snowstorm. Shadow was chained to his doghouse in the Fullers' yard when he managed to slip out of his collar.

The collie, who had never wandered far from home before, apparently became disoriented at the beginning of the storm. When Judy went out the next morning, the doghouse was empty.

Judy alerted neighbors, the police, the mailman and the local dog catcher. Then she spent the entire day scouring the neighborhood, which is located less than a mile from the bay.

When Judy's 12-year-old son Richard got home from school, he joined the search. At dusk, they returned home for flashlights and went out again. The wind chill factor that night was 50 below zero.

For the next 18 days, the Fuller family staged a massive and expensive search. They placed advertisements in the Press-Gazette and posters in local stores, offering a $100 reward.

When they received calls from people who had seen a collie, they jumped in their jeep and drove to the scene, running up a $100 gasoline bill in the process.

Judy went on the radio in an attempt to locate a man who had telephoned with information, but failed

☐ Shadow's home

Shadow. How could a blind dog get clear across the bay and 10 miles inland to boot?

Of course, the dog inside *was* Shadow. Although ill with pneumonia, weak and lighter by 25 pounds, the collie recognized the Fullers and there was an exuberant and tearful reunion.

These days, Shadow sticks close to home. In fact, he seldom leaves the family, constantly begging to be petted, or trying to climb onto someone's lap.

Although the Fullers own seven other dogs, Judy was mystified when asked the obvious question: Why spend so much time and money searching for one?

"He's our responsibility," she said simply. "We couldn't let him wander around."

As soon as Shadow recovers, the Fullers plan to housebreak him. From now on, the yard dog will be a house dog.

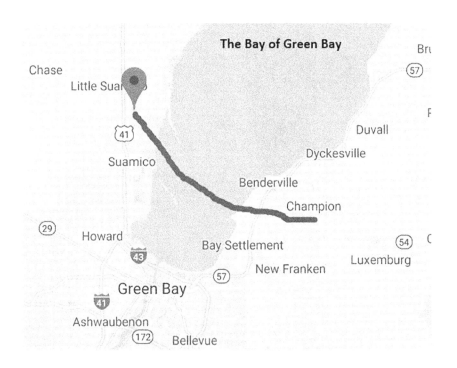

Shadow's Journey

Ti

Ti, a lovable, old golden retriever, had become disoriented and wandered away from home. Lost, he was unable to find his way back. It was a hot July day, and he was searching for water to quench his thirst and help him cool off. As he came up to the East River, it looked like the perfect place to walk down, get a drink, and jump back up; but when Ti tried to jump back up the bank, his hind legs just sank farther into the mud. Exhausted, he tried to lie down; but the water crept up his chest, inch by inch, so Ti had a choice: he could sit back up or lie down and drown.

Ti was probably thinking, *Where is David? I wish he'd come looking for me*. Little did Ti know that David already had one of the best search-and-rescue teams out looking for him. Gary, Laurie, their three girls, and I had worked as a team for years looking for other people's lost dogs. The dogs that we really focused on were the old ones like Ti— dogs that had become disoriented and headed home the wrong way.

Back in the 1990s, during an average week, fifteen to twenty dogs were reported lost to the Bay Area Humane Society in Green Bay. By the time Ti was lost, it had been almost fifteen years since I started analyzing why dogs were lost. I had determined that, other than through plain carelessness, the majority of them were lost for one of four reasons:

1. They were very old and had become disoriented.
2. They were being watched by someone other than their owner (sometimes even at the dog's home), or they had a new owner.
3. They were young, unneutered male dogs.

19

4.	They ran away because they were frightened by a loud noise such as fireworks, gunshots, or cars backfiring.

The very old ones like Ti created the most anxiety because they were usually cherished family pets—pets that had never left the yard before. For fifteen years, I had heard remarkably similar statements from the owners of lost old dogs: "She would never leave the yard. She can't even walk more than a block."

We find many of them blocks and even miles from home. Some owners are so insistent that their dogs won't leave the yard that I find myself wanting to say, "Well then, no problem. She must be in your yard someplace," but then empathy takes over; and I hear the anxiety in their voices.

Many younger adults, usually men, start their first phone call to me with the words, "My three-year-old really misses the dog." The second day, it changes to, "We've just got to find her." By the third day, it's, "She's a part of our family." It's often the men I converse with because the women are so emotionally distraught they are unable to make the call.

As a canine-rescue team, we hear these statements every day. It isn't every day that a person loses a pet. This is a new and stressful experience for them, and most people don't know that there are many places to call in addition to the humane societies. Additional places to contact include highway departments, town chairmen, and constables. Town chairmen in mostly rural areas appoint a constable to oversee minor legal matters. If you are living in a rural community, who are these people and where do you find their phone numbers?

My favorite animal-welfare mentor, Dr. Sam Vainisi, clued me in to the fact that old dogs and cats are like old people. Dogs become disoriented, become lost, and can go for miles. Thus, people came to believe one of the old myths, "They go away to die." I found that the really old ones usually go in a straight line. My theory is that they make two turns instead of three, or else they go too far before they make the third turn, and they overshoot their regular path or routine and just keep going. Younger dogs seem to circle when they get lost. The signs are so successful that we can tell what path the dog is taking by monitoring when and where the phone calls come from.

Advice and help from the local humane societies regarding lost dogs vary depending on the size of their staff. Many of the staff are overworked and underpaid, so it can be an ideal project for good, long-term volunteers who can work outside the box such as we did. It's not easy to concentrate on helping people find their lost pets when you have dozens of pleading eyes right there at the shelter looking for attention.

The day after Ti went missing, Timber, our best bird dog, and I checked all the secluded areas where it would be possible for Ti to be without someone seeing him. There were long grasses and brush behind a strip mall, around a grade school, and down next to a branch of the East River. The day was hot and humid, so Ti was probably lying down in the shade someplace. Luckily, Timber had all the possible areas checked out before noon.

Today was the third day Ti was missing, still no calls. I had fine-tuned the lost-dog signs by now. For some strange reason, no one was seeing him. Where could he be? My thoughts went back to a song that my sisters and I sang when we were little, "Where, oh, where has my little dog gone?"

The East River, a tributary of the Fox River, was just blocks away from Ti's home. The river haunted me. My mind drifted back to the question, "Where is Ti?" The previous year, one of our searches led to a dead dog floating in the river. Would this be the same situation for Ti? Or would he be able to get to and from the water, and we'd eventually find him happily dozing on a patch of grass? Being an eternal optimist led me to make the decision to search for that patch of grass.

On the third day, Gary and Laurie started out searching for Ti with their red setter, Bailey. I was going to join them later. Usually, one of their three daughters went with us. All three girls were troopers, so we were disappointed when none of them could join the search. Instead, we comforted ourselves with the fact that Bailey could make up for their loss. Little did we know how true that would be.

Bailey had been with us on many treks, some successful strictly because of Bailey. Just to watch him was a joy. A magnificent deep-red setter, he was big and tall and moved swiftly and quietly through the long grass and weeds. His favorite prey was pheasants, but he was excited and happy just to be out in the fields.

Gary's thoughts were, *if Ti came out from his cul-de-sac, which is only a block long, he would have to turn right or left. If he turned right and went straight, he'd go right to the river. If he turned left, he would hit a busy street, and surely someone would have seen him and called, so we took the route to the right.*

Once Gary and Laurie got to the river, it looked as if it would be easier to go to the left, so they headed in that direction. In that particular area, no one would see the dog unless they were right next to him because of all the cattails and brush. Gary and Laurie stayed as close to the water as they could with the expectation of seeing a floating dead dog. Bailey, however, was more optimistic in doing his usual thing—checking out the smells and underneath the piles of brush, pausing at things most people wouldn't see. We were confident but not optimistic that he would spot things that we wouldn't even notice because a lot of brush was rust colored, just like Bailey.

Covering almost four hundred yards, Gary and Laurie came to an area where homes backed up to the water where people might notice a stray dog. They knew that people would be out in their backyards at this time of the year, and they thought that surely the kids would be playing by the water.

They were ready to give up the search and turn around, but then Bailey started acting excited. Gary decided to take one last look over the edge of the bank. For a moment, he couldn't believe his eyes. Was he imagining what he was seeing? Lying in the water right below him was a golden retriever!

"My God, Laurie, come here!" Laurie rushed to join Gary.

It's as if it were yesterday. I can still hear Gary telling what happened next.

"I stumbled and slid down the bank as quickly as I could. Emotionally and physically drained from the walk in the heat, I plunked right down next to Ti. What a great example of this magnificent breed he was, gray muzzle and all. He was very quiet as I assessed the situation. It was obvious that he couldn't stand."

"I stroked his head and assured him that he was safe and that we were there to help. Looking at the high bank behind him, I wondered how I would get back up there with him in my arms. Big, old, chunky goldens were not the lightest dogs to get up a steep five-foot embankment. It was worth a try; and with one fell swoop, I charged up the bank with Ty in my arms."

"Even at the top on level ground, Ti could not stand. But surely, he would be okay. What was I thinking? He *had* to be okay."

"The closest vet clinic was only several blocks away; but first, we had to get him to the van, which was yards away. Ti hadn't missed many meals, and it was a struggle every step of the way. Panting with the heat, I had to stop and rest several times."

Finally, a muddy Gary laid a muddy Ti in the van, and Laurie knelt down beside him, assuring him he was now safe and going home.

The veterinarian's words were crushing. "Too long in the water. Water burn, shutting down." Not ready to give up, Gary called me. After all this, we couldn't just put him down. We decided to get another opinion. One from Dr. Steve De Grave, a veterinarian we both used for our own dogs. Dr. Steve saw us within minutes.

Gary stumbled out to the van with Ti in his arms. We all hung on to every word and trusted Dr. Steve completely. His comments were guarded, "Intravenous fluids." Again he said, "Too long in the water. Water burn. Try for twenty-four hours." The waiting period would give us all time to adjust and accept reality.

It was a long night. Seven thirty in the morning, the time for the clinic to open, couldn't come fast enough. Mercifully, Dr. Steve called at seven forty-five. "Good news," he said. "He can stand up, and he's wagging his tail."

Reunions are always emotional, but this one was special. No scene can be more rewarding than a graying, waterlogged fourteen-year-old golden retriever and his tearful owner.

Ti

THE GREEN BAY NEWS-CHRONICLE LOCAL

A nose for finding lost dogs

A De Pere man and his canine companion help reunite families when dogs and cats wander

By Christopher Clough
The News-Chronicle

Gary Zehms takes Bailey, his 5-year-old red setter, grouse hunting with him on weekends.

But sometimes Gary and Bailey track down more land-bound creatures.

As part of the volunteer Animal Rescue Group, they are called upon to sniff out runaway pets.

"We go looking for dogs over the age of 10," Zehms said, "or dogs lost in more of a country setting, fields, woods, where they could be anywhere and visibility is not as good."

Situations like that are where Bailey is most helpful, where a dog's nose can sense what human eyes might miss.

"Dogs like to find things," Zehms said. "The nose is all instinct. We give them a blanket or something the pet laid on just before it ran away so it has the scent."

He has been doing this about three years, when he met group leader Bette Anderson as she was selling him his De Pere home.

Since then, Zehms, Anderson and other volunteers, working as a team, have gone out with their tracking dogs about six to eight times a year to locate stray pets.

Once the group has been called, the first thing they do is talk with the pet's owners.

"The more we know about the pet and its habits, the better," Zehms said. "Does it like to chase things, does it like to run near the creek, what are its tendencies?"

Next is letting the owner's neighbors know they're there and getting permission to be on their land.

They also put up signs in case the pet has been sighted on the loose.

After that, it's time to "release the hounds."

Bailey didn't need more schooling to make the transition from hunting grouse to seeking lost pets.

"My dog is a pointing dog. There's an indication when he's found something," Zehms said. "He actually hasn't come up and pointed right at (a stray), but I know the difference between when he's just looking around and when he's on the scent."

Finding a runaway animal in a hay field might seem, well, like finding a needle in a haystack. But considering the wide open spaces he, Bailey and the other volunteers work in, Zehms thinks they've beaten the odds.

"It's been surprisingly good. (My team) has been successful maybe six out of 10 times," he said.

said. "Sometimes we find a dog that's been killed, but at least it gives the owner some closure."

Most of the pets Zehms and Bailey look for are dogs, with only the occasional feline thrown in.

"(Cats) are a lot more difficult," Zehms said. "Dogs are out there running around in the open, while cats like to hide."

Many of them are elderly. Dogs and cats over 8 years old may not run away as much as they get disoriented while loose and just wander around lost.

Zehms said the best thing pet owners can do when they discover their furry friend has disappeared is notify the humane society immediately.

"Some owners don't want us out there, don't want signs posted," he said. "There's a stigma about dogs running away just to find a place to die, and it's an emotional roller coaster during that time.

"The sooner we know and the sooner we get out there, the better. If it's not reported for three or four days, there are a lot of directions the animal could have wandered off in that time."

Christopher Clough / The News-Chronicle

GARY ZEHMS AND HIS 5-year-old setter, Bailey, are an animal rescue team who help locate lost pets.

Gary Zehms and "Bailey"

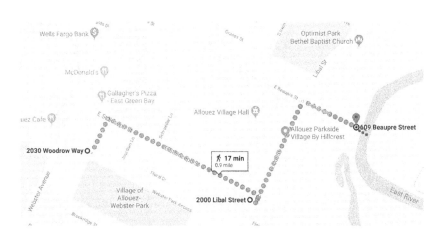

Ti's journey

Ophy

The scream of a siren. Flashing red lights. Darn, was I speeding again? "Geeze, Bette," Bob exclaimed. "What in the hell are you doing out on a night like this?" Thinking back, it was pretty darn cold. About twenty degrees below zero. A little crunchy walking on the snow.

Bob Olsen, a state cop and longtime friend of my husband, Emmy peered into my car, probably to make sure it was me. It was, after all, a good night for stealing cars. A lot of people left them running while they ran into a gas station or grocery store to stock up on snacks before taking refuge from the nasty weather.

"Some old hunting dog is lost in this area, Bob," I said. "A guy who lives in Green Bay was taking him for a walk in the woods by the airport in Oconto. His dog was losing its hearing and couldn't hear his owner's call. More than likely, the dog is trying to find its way home."

My friend Patsy Rowley and I were out doing the best thing possible for Ophy, the lost dog. We were putting up signs. Hopefully, the signs would have everyone in the area looking for him. It was a long hike from the airport in Oconto to the suburbs of Green Bay—about thirty miles, all country with no towns. If people were out, they were more than likely going to and from work. It was too cold to do anything else even for the cross-country skiers and snowmobilers.

Bob sent us on our way but not before we made him promise to watch for Ophy. I had complete faith in him because he was a consummate animal lover and a top-notch dog trainer, specializing in hunting dogs. You couldn't have better eyes than his looking for a dog. If only he had been on a day schedule that week because more than likely, Ophy was hunkered down for the night when it was the coldest. Later, however, I changed my mind on that idea.

As it turned out, Ophy's beginning was not the best to make him an ideal candidate to trust strangers. That's a major disadvantage for any dog if it becomes lost. Ironically, it was an act of cruelty that led him to end up in a great dog-friendly home. The story as I know it, started out when Ophy was just a puppy.

Young Mary Blindauer and her friend Sue were meandering down a secluded railroad track that ran right through a residential area close to Mary's home. It wasn't something that they often did; but thank goodness, they did that day. When Mary and Sue approached a cardboard box sitting right on the tracks, Sue spotted something in the open box. Who would have believed it? It was a living, moving puppy, hardly old enough to leave its mother.

"At first, we thought the puppy was dirty," Mary said, "but after we looked closely, we thought it might be grease. We were so excited. We could hardly wait to get the puppy home."

"My father thought it was some kind of petroleum product on the puppy because years ago, some people put petroleum on a dog to get rid of ringworm. A visit to the Ashwaubenon Veterinary Clinic in Green Bay debunked that theory. The puppy didn't have ringworm."

Mary continued, "Obviously, with the dog coming from a bad home, my father decided that the puppy shouldn't go back. Lucky me. We decided that Ophy, standing for orphan, would be a good name for him. From then on, he was my constant companion. However, there never was any question that his real loyalty was to my father for the rest of his life. My father was the only man Ophy really liked and trusted. He even guarded my father's workroom and wouldn't let any of us kids in. Actually, that was a good thing because my father was in the heating business, and there were expensive parts and tools in his workroom. Ophy did let my brother, Pat, take him for walks, though probably only because they both loved the woods."

One of those walks took place when the rest of the family was on a skiing vacation out of town. Ophy took off on a deer and didn't respond to Pat's calls or whistle. Unfortunately, they were near the Oconto airport, which was thirty miles from home.

Pat's call to the Humane Society in Green Bay got Ophy's name on the special attention list because of his age. Ophy was thirteen years old. The lost-dog rescue group quickly went into action.

Shortly after a week passed, Pat received an encouraging call that someone had spotted a red and white dog walking along Airport Road. That was one of the roads Ophy would have traveled going from the airport toward Green Bay. It made sense because there was a lot of snow, and we felt that Ophy would be traveling close to the road or else holed up close to the road surrounded by some woods or brush. We felt his red spots would stand out if anyone got close enough to him. Friends and animal lovers—Cathy, Patsy, and Julie— all spent hours driving the area in the frigid weather. Successes, in the extreme cold in the past, were almost a necessity for the volunteers to keep searching. Usually, the owners of lost dogs would take off work to search with us, sometimes for days and sometimes the whole time their pets were missing.

A week passed, Patsy and I discussed the possibility of Ophy being at a Class-B animal dealer, south of Green Bay. Class-B animal dealers were licensed by the USDA to collect random (i.e., stray and unwanted) dogs to sell to laboratories for research purposes. The year was 1989, and the Class-B animal dealer we were thinking of was not forced to surrender his license until 1994. Both Patsy and I were working extensively on forcing the issue of that animal dealer losing his license. We wondered if there were *bunchers* in the Oconto area. It was one of our biggest fears, more than the temperature of negative twenty degrees. Men called *bunchers* collected dogs for Class-B animal dealers (dogs obtained at random) and were paid meager sums. The Class-B animal dealers collected considerably more for the random dogs from the medical schools than what they paid the bunchers. We were aware the open records for the USDA showed that a local animal dealer sold them 27,868 dogs from 1972 through 1989. Yes, that's right. A despicable way to make a living. I always questioned where the research dogs were collected from. Wisconsin medical schools discontinued buying animals from Class-B animal dealers after this dealer lost is license.

Two weeks passed. There were no more calls. The rescue team started comparing Judy and George's lost Shadow situation to Ophy. The weather was frigid both times. Both dogs were lost in a country setting, and they were both collie mixes. We prayed the ending would be similar. This gave us hope. Ophy had one big advantage: he wasn't blind, but he was thirteen years old while Shadow was only two. We hung on to every little detail that might keep our spirits up.

Another trait made Ophy similar to Shadow: no one was seeing either of them. To both the inexperienced or new searchers, this would be a big downer because they would probably assume that the dog was dead; but for us, it could mean that they both traveled at night when no one could see them, or it was quieter with fewer cars on the road or perhaps instinct told them to move when it was colder because the chance of freezing to death was less if they were moving. These questions and thoughts always came up with missing Shelties because they were seen the least when they were lost. Collies are often similar to shelties in personality and actions; therefore, we thought they might react the same way.

One morning, right out of the blue, I got a call.

"I've got Ophy!" It was Pat. It was the sixteenth day, and Ophy finally made it home. His nails were just stubs, and his teeth were worn down. What had he tried to eat? We had never seen that before. Raw and bloody paws along with worn-down nails were common but not badly worn teeth. The only thing we could think of was that Ophy existed by eating something very hard or frozen. Possibly, road kill such as a dead rabbit or deer.

Ophy had ended up at a little house along a road named, of all things, Chicken Shack Road. The woman couldn't remember whether he had been eating with the birds for three or four days before she saw our signs. However, many days, it was didn't matter to Ophy. He was ready to go home.

Ophy

Ophy

Ophy's Journey

Ophy

Angel

It was Christmas time in Wisconsin. A pretty time of the year, especially in the country. A wreath on every door and even on some barns, Christmas tree lights twinkling on the evergreen trees, and quaint narrow roads lined with freshly plowed snow. There wasn't much room on those roads for a stubby little collie to trot and still miss the cars rushing past. She did though. All winter, she traveled those same roads. What and who was she looking for? Who did she belong to?

This little collie wasn't much bigger than a cocker spaniel. She appeared alone on those same roads in the spring. Everyone wondered about her, but no one stopped.

One day, she was spotted holding a puppy in her mouth. A car stopped, then a second car. The little dog dropped the puppy and darted into a patch of woods nearby. She was probably looking on as the driver got out of her car and picked up the little lifeless puppy. Not wanting the dog to go any farther and get lost, the woman gently put it down and tried calling the dog, but the dog ran deeper and deeper into the woods.

The woman got back into her car and drove off. The other car did the same. The first driver often wondered about the little dog. She even called the local animal shelter, but they had not received any calls about a dog missing from that area.

Across the field where the lady had seen the dog, a deserted house echoed sadness. The elderly man who used to live there died just before Christmas. He had lived alone—or so most people thought.

Once he died, everything on the property was auctioned off except the house. Everything went but the little dog. No one seemed to realize that she belonged to the house. Surely, she must have been around at times during the auction. Someone had probably called to her, but she was shy and not one to trust strangers. Eventually, there was nothing left but the empty house and the dog. Spring faded into summer, and still the little collie walked along those same country roads.

Fall arrived, and people still saw her wandering about. It had been almost a year. People who saw her wondered whether she looked thinner. She was often talked about, but it was hard to tell how thin she was with her thick, fluffy coat.

She still trotted along those same roads. From Christmas through the next fall. She was just a part of the scene.

In September, the home was auctioned off. Even though it was in need of repair and had a dilapidated shed that needed to be torn down, Sue just loved the old house, so she and her husband bought it. She had known the old man. They often had him for Christmas because he seemed to be so alone. He did have some small poo-dle-type dogs, which seemed to be his only company. Sue was glad that the property's old barn had burned down a long time ago. There would be enough work that needed to be done to the house without having to worry about a barn. Sue and her family lived only a few miles away and had seen the property slowly deteriorate.

They saw the dog the first weekend they visited the property. Thinking it belonged to the neighbors, they shooed her away, fearing she'd be hit by a car. They didn't want to encourage her running back and forth.

One weekend, Sue and her family came to spend time at the house; and they saw the dog again. Sue decided it had to belong to someone in the area; but when Sue was walking by the old shed later in the afternoon, she thought she heard something. Squeaking. Crying. Yipping. She stopped and listened. It sounded like puppies! Puppies crying? It couldn't be! But it sure sounded like it.

Sue squeezed herself very carefully halfway into the shed and stopped, unable to believe her eyes. Puppies! Could it really be? It was! Puppies, adorable puppies wrestling, jumping, and playing. Six of them, all black and white. None of them looked like the little collie. Although the dog was watching Sue very closely, she wouldn't come into the old building. Surely, she must be the puppies' mother. Who did the mother dog belong to? Why were the puppies here at this vacant house?

After checking with some of the neighbors, Sue learned, as radio personality Paul Harvey used to say, the rest of the story.

The little collie did belong to someone. That someone had been the old man who had lived in Sue's newly acquired house. He'd died in December of 1989. It was now September of 1990. The dog had wandered alone for nine months and had two litters of puppies.

What would she do about the dog and the puppies? Sue and her family had no plans to live in the house until it was fully renovated. What could she do about the dog?

Sue called her sister-in-law, Norma, in Green Bay. Norma's *found report* was directed to her friend Bette, who lived in De Pere.

The job of finding a home for this orphaned family fell to me. I contacted George and Judy Fuller and met them the next day. George and Judy were my longtime friends and worked with me to help rescue animals. After a flurry of phone calls, the three of us drove to the little country village of Angelica.

Arriving at the old shed, we began to load the puppies into crates. The mother dog stood off in the field watching. Always watching. Unsocialized puppies are not easy to catch if they are old enough to run fast, but George and Judy were experts. They confined the puppies in such a way that they had no escape route. Usually, a mother dog, if she isn't feral, will go into a crate with her puppies but not this time. George and Judy tried every trick in their arsenal before they gave up and headed for Green Bay's Humane Society with their precious cargo of puppies. Fortunately, the babies were old enough to eat on their own. Now the job of getting the mother dog became our top priority. Clouds had formed overhead, so we knew a storm was brewing. We knew that getting the frightened mother dog would be a challenge. One of the bystanders suggested we use a tranquilizer gun to stun her. For a person who watches enough animal shows on television, that would be an understandable suggestion. Television shows make darting and catching an animal look easy and safe. They show only the successful scenarios. It is neither easy nor always safe to tranquilize animals, especially small animals.

Mike Reed, the director of the Green Bay Wildlife Sanctuary, had educated me well on tranquilizer guns. One has to take into account the amount of the tranquilizer to use, access to the necessary angle to inject it, the animal's reaction after being injected, how far that animal can run before the tranquilizer takes effect, the weather, and other variables. There is always a possibility for a darted and terrified animal to run into traffic or a pond or a river or deep in the woods, which makes it difficult to find it in time especially if the rescue is being attempted in very cold weather. We thought our best option would be to trap her.

We borrowed a trap and set it the next day using cat food as bait. We added a smoke-flavored enhancer to the cat food to make sure the smell would be as effective as possible. Fortunately, Sue agreed to check the trap regularly. Together, we worried about the upcoming storm. Maybe the dog wouldn't go into the trap. That was a possibility. Every day, Sue checked the trap.

Sue finally called. "She's in the trap." It took six days, six long days. Finally! We felt so thankful and so happy that the mother dog could be reunited with her puppies. It was at that point we decided to call her Angel.

Angel was reunited with her babies at the shelter later that morning. Both Angel and especially her puppies seemed to enjoy their new home and all the accompanying attention. She carefully checked each one, and then they all settled in for a long nap. It was a scene one would not soon forget.

It didn't take long for each adorable puppy to find a perfect home, but would anyone ever want Angel? This is the typical shelter scene throughout the country. Potential new owners never seem to be looking for large black dogs, old dogs, or mother dogs who are sad and depressed because they have lost their puppies. It's easy to understand why so many good animal-care workers in a shelter last only a year or two. Fortunately for Angel, George and Judy kept checking on her status at the shelter.

They had already told all their friends and coworkers about the sad and stubby little collie. Judy convinced her good friend Wendy and her husband, Dan, to stop in and at least see her. It didn't take long for them to realize that George and Judy were right. Angel would be a perfect addition to their family. As quickly as the application was approved, Angel was finally on her way home.

Angel adapted to her new home and the other pets quickly. She never once had an accident in the house. She didn't ask for much, just a little space to curl up close to Wendy's or Dan's chair.

She probably didn't even know that she was pampered, but she was—for the rest of her life.

Angel

"ANGEL"

ANGEL was owned by a farmer who died in December 1989. Everything at the farm which was located in Shawano County was auctioned off last summer. The new owner did not move in but recently saw Angel and thinking she was a neighborhood dog tried to shoo her back home. The second time she was near a building and they heard puppy cries. A recent investigation found that Angel has searched for food in the surrounding area all that time. Now she and her puppies are safe and well fed, waiting for that new home!

Sheba

Sheba was missing.

"Blind, old, railroad tracks nearby." These were just some of the snippets about Sheba that kept running through my head. Lost dogs had a habit of capturing every spare minute of my mind when I wasn't working or sleeping.

Some dogs just naturally bring joy into our lives. Sheba was one, and I would eventually find that out for myself. She was just a puppy when Carol and Vernon got her, an adorable little puff of gray. Now a typical aging keeshond, she had that curled-up tail, which was always wagging. Her coat was a dense gray with some black, and she still had those perky little ears that stood straight up. Her muzzle was turning gray; and sadly, she had been blind for a long time. Thankfully, it didn't seem to affect her as much as it did everyone else.

Normally tied up when she was outside, Sheba had somehow slipped her tie out and disappeared. What a place to be lost! Close to Carol and Vernon's home, there was an iced-over river with patches of open water, a large wooded area where she could easily disappear, and a heavily traveled highway running in front of the house. If that weren't bad enough, there were railroad tracks running next to the house. Admittedly, it was a pretty bleak assessment.

Although it was winter, it wasn't especially cold. We were grateful that Sheba's thick coat would compensate for the season. We also had another advantage. There was enough snow to make tracking easy.

With all the other strikes against her, time was of the essence. Lost-dog signs went up within hours, and the search started the next day. Vernon was not well, and Carol worked her job during daylight hours. Therefore, I enlisted my friend Sue Engberg to help again with the search.

The day I put up the signs, I covered the area in back of Vernon's house myself. The dog tracks, which were probably Sheba's, went back about 150 feet. The only tracks I saw led to the house. There were a few bare spots that later proved to be important. The next day Sue and I headed toward the river, which wasn't that far away. It was always an anxious time when we checked rivers, ponds, and lakes. Water is very unforgiving, and an old dog doesn't stand much of a chance in icy water. I had seen the right size hole in the ice more than once before; but when I investigated, we never found the dog. At least the ending would have been mercifully quick.

Relieved after not finding any suspicious breaks in the ice, we headed for the wooded area across the road. There were clusters of trees; and every so often, there were open snow-covered areas. Sue found one open site with crisscrossing tracks leading into the woods. On closer examination, we could see that the tracks had to be from a younger animal or animals, perhaps a fox or coyote. The tracks were much farther apart, more like an animal running would make. We knew they definitely were not the short tracks of an old dog walking.

We took a break from trudging the heavy snow for several hours by driving around within a two-mile radius, checking the sides and shoulders of roads. It wouldn't be the first time we found a dog that way, curled up next to the highway, exhausted but alive and just napping. But no Sheba.

Next to the patches of the woods was a school with a big open recreational area in the back that led to more trees. There were no footprints across the whole section. What a relief that was because it would have been a huge area to cover.

Thinking back to the first day, when I had searched the backyard of the owner's home and saw only the tracks that were probably hers, I decided to spend more time on that side of the road. I needed to be certain that no dog tracks went any farther or on either side of the road off the bare spots where there would be no tracks at all.

It seemed like a perfect area for me to enlist Timber's help in the search. Timber was one of my husband's well-trained hunting dogs.

There was no open water. There were no cars. That concern had been drilled into me. "Be careful with the dogs," I was told. Meaning, "Don't send the dogs into an area that's not safe." The railroad tracks were a concern, but I had checked the train schedule, and it would be hours before the next train went through. Not surprising, I was warned that the tracks were on private property. Being the daughter of a railroad man, I understood.

Timber, a small liver-and-white springer, was at her finest that day. She was happy to get out and run, and her tail never stopped wagging. She was from a third generation litter that we had and was pretty spoiled; but out in the field, she was all business.

We were out less than an hour when Timber went down a slight incline and headed for a cluster of brush close to the tracks. She stopped and looked back at me. Her tail stopped, and she crunched down. I yelled at her to stop because I suspected an opossum was hiding there, and I didn't want her to get into a tussle with it. Opossums have powerful teeth that can be tough on a dog. As I got closer to the area, I could see it looked like an animal of some kind, probably dead. It was dark colored, so I knew it wasn't a coyote. A darker wolf came to mind, but I didn't know whether there were any in that area. Just then, Timber barked, and two perky little ears popped up. It was Sheba! I called her name, and Timber wagged her tail furiously. I yelled, "Stay." Timber dropped to the ground. Sheba stood up, which was a good sign. At my age, I was in no condition to carry her. I approached Sheba and knelt down. She wagged her tail as I stroked her head. "Good girl, Sheba!" I said as she took a couple of steps toward me. Timber, however, remained in the down position as she had been trained. It was obvious she realized she *had her bird*, and she was pleased with herself. I repeated the words *good girl* to Timber a couple of times so she would know she had accomplished her goal.

Resting every so often, for both my sake and Sheba's, we finally arrived back at Vernon's home. Carol and Vernon weren't even aware that Timber and I had been searching for Sheba that day. I knocked on the door. Carol opened it. There, the three of us stood. It was a very happy reunion.

Sheba remained in my life after her rescue. Recently, retired from real estate, I had planned on joining a fitness program of some type. It occurred to me that day that maybe what Sheba and I both needed were long walks. I was right. Every day we went out, we had a wonderful time. Snowstorms, subzero weather, thunderstorms, and then the heat. I picked up Sheba every day for over a year, then Vernon died. Carol moved because the home was slated to be demolished for new road construction. Luckily, Sharon—a good friend of mine—wanted to take Sheba, who was almost thirteen years old at that time. Sharon lived much closer to me, so I was still able to see Sheba on a frequent basis. In this last chapter of Sheba's life, she had a wonderful fenced yard to roam in and the companionship of a greyhound named Ambi.

Old age took over after a wonderful year in her new home. Sheba died, but my memory of her lingers on. Her photo remains with me in a little silver frame that has captured a special spot in my home. I smile at Sheba every time I walk by.

Sheba

Sheba and Timber

Timber, Sheba, and Carol Cornelius

Schneider

The semi roared by. What the heck was that between the cab and the trailer? A dog? It couldn't be! But it was. Ears down, legs braced, standing on the platform between the cab and the trailer, frozen with fear.

A closer look would have revealed the massive injury taking place at that moment. Blood oozed from the area where the drive shaft rotated on the dog's flank. The pain had to be excruciating, but the dog was smart enough to know that a jump down between those big wheels would mean certain death.

How long could she stand the pain? At least the lightning couldn't reach her where she was, but when would those jagged flashes of lightning stop? This had to be one of the worst days of any dog's life, especially this one.

Unaware of their new passenger, Tom Van Den Elzen and Bob Biemeret—longtime employees of Schneider National Trucking in Green Bay, Wisconsin—had just settled in for the final leg of the trip home. Having ridden through stormy weather for most of the trip, they had a clear shot now. There wasn't another stop scheduled after they passed through the village of Pound. Green Bay was only forty-five miles away.

It had been a long day, and both men were tired. With a sigh of relief, Tom pulled into the Schneider parking lot. Coming around the cab, Tom couldn't believe his eyes. Was that a dog? What was a dog doing there? A better look made it clear to the two men what the story was. For some reason, a dog had jumped up and landed on the platform called the fifth wheel, the section between the cab and the trailer. As the truck moved, the drive shaft severely injured the dog.

Smart and in her prime, the dog had been able to hold on for the rest of the trip.

They put in a call to the De Pere Police Department. The animal hospital callback quickly followed. When they arrived at the animal clinic, the veterinarian examined the injured animal. The German shepherd's story is one that has happened hundreds of times to dogs all over the United States. Over the years, I have come to the conclusion that this dog must have gotten on before Pound or had run a long distance from the west or north before it jumped up on the platform. Had there been a Humane Society in Oconto, someone might have called regarding a missing dog. However, no organization existed there yet, which didn't help the situation because there are very few people who check for their lost pets in surrounding counties.

Another scenario is that stray dogs may not always go to the shelter. In outlying areas, stray dogs may go to someone assigned the responsibility of caring for them. In Wisconsin, that person could be a constable, who may not be responsible for taking dogs to the shelter. Constables may just keep them, find another home for them, or have them put down.

The responsibility of having a dog properly identified is always the owner's. Tags or microchips or both belong on every pet.

It would be a long recovery. Dr. Wayne Hill was the perfect person to take charge. Patient, kind, and very experienced, he was convinced that there was an owner out there looking for such a nice dog. As I was a longtime client of Dr. Wayne's and a volunteer for the Humane Society, he called me the next day for help finding the dog's owner.

Bob and Tom thought back to where the dog could have hitched the ride. Neither of them could think of any stop they had made, not even for a stop sign after they passed through the village of Pound. That was forty-five miles away! They figured she must have jumped on at Pound or shortly before.

I went into *lost-dog mode*, only this time in reverse. Who would people call if they were missing a dog in that area? The sheriff's department, the local police, the constables, and the veterinarians. I contacted them all but had no luck. We extended our search area.

The *Green Bay Press Gazette* ran an article with a photo, and the Bay Area Humane Society showed the dog on a local television station. Still no response.

The publicity did not result in finding the owner, but it did result in finding the dog a wonderful new home. Christi George's mother saw the news broadcast and called Christi. After a month at the animal hospital and a stay in foster care, the dog was finally going to her new home. Not surprising, the new owners named this fortunate survivor *Schneider* after her harrowing ride with Schneider Truck Transport.

We will never know why no one was looking for Schneider, but that was fine with the Georges. Schneider loved everyone, and everyone loved her. Her greatest joy was playing with a Frisbee. If necessary, she'd even climb a tree to retrieve one; but the trauma had left its mark on Schneider. She never got over her fear of storms. During one thunderstorm at her new home, she jumped out a window. Her new owners eventually found her ten miles away.

Although the fur never grew back on Schneider's side, the injury healed completely; and she eventually died of old age.

The following poem was written by Christi a long time ago and is a fitting tribute to a dog that fought the battle to live and won.

To Schneider
by Christi George

It was an honor to have known you.
We're so glad you chose to stay.
You changed our lives completely
With your gentle, dignified way.

I know God has a Frisbee saved
Especially for you
So once again you can jump
And fly through the sky of blue.

No pain you will be feeling
As you race and run and play.
Your angel will take care of you
And throw your Frisbee every day.

And here, we'll shed some tears,
But mostly, we will smile.
For the best we have known
Even if for just a while.

So good-bye for now, our special one,
Until we meet again.
For now we'll cherish each moment we had
And our love shall never end.

Schneider with new owner, Dennis George

SCHNEIDER HITCHHIKER

Wedged in the area where the trailer hooks up to the cab on a semi, this lucky little Shepherd dog rode at least 80 miles last weekend from the northern part of the state.

Evidently scared by a storm and unnoticed by the driver, "Schneider" ran for cover and ended up between the drive shaft and the power takeoff pump. Severely burned on the flank by the rotation of the drive shaft, she was discovered on arrival in Green Bay and rescued by Schneider National driver, Tom Van Den Elzen and mechanic, Bob Biemeret (shown in picture). Treated by a local vet and still under care, "Schneider" will be fine but needs your help.

If you can, please send money for "Schneider's" care to the Humane Society at 2206 N. Quincy St., Green Bay, WI 54302 and mark the envelope "Schneider".

"Schneider" may need a home also — would you be interested in really making this her "lucky day"?

Schneider

Schneider

Schneider's Journey

Chester

Lost hundreds of miles from home, Chester wasn't looking for a house. He was looking for his truck. It belonged to him and James, and home for both of them was in Fort Wayne, Indiana.

Truckers and their companion dogs are seen all over the United States. Big dogs, little *yappers*, and guard dogs, you're bound to see almost anything sitting next to the driver. We had searched for missing trucker dogs before. We had looked for another one for three weeks before he came back to the truck stop in Bellevue. He was a *little yapper* that weighed less than twenty pounds. The signs we had posted were the reason for success that time. Hopefully our signs would work again.

It became apparent to me that a trucker's dog was as important to the driver as a hunting dog was to a hunter. Driving cross-country, after all, is a lonely business.

Chester was in his regular spot in the cab when the truck pulled up to the paper mill on Quincy Street in Green Bay. Chester scrambled out of the truck when James got out, and he took off. No amount of calling or whistling could coax him to come back. James needed to be on his way home, and though he didn't want to leave without his dog, he notified the Bay Area Humane Society within hours of Chester's escape, and they placed Chester on the top-priority list. Remorsefully, James headed home.

The Bay Area Humane Society contacted me immediately, and the signs went up within hours. We started getting calls about Chester within an hour. He was heading south, away from the mill. That was worrisome because we were afraid he was heading home toward Indiana. People approached him; and even though he didn't appear spooked, he was not interested in treats, food, or people. Chester was on a mission.

He was heading south on Webster Avenue, a street with heavy traffic. Our first caller reported him walking past the two hospitals in a very busy traffic area. Farther south on Webster, people reported that Chester started checking out the streets that went to the left. Then coming back to Webster Avenue, he'd go south again on the next street to the left for a while before returning to Webster Avenue again.

We had once tracked an old hound by the name of Spook. He'd done the same thing years before in the country area of Little Suamico, where he lived. Spook finally found his way home, but it wouldn't work for Chester who was hundreds of miles from home.

The calls kept coming in. We were puzzled that when strangers approached Chester, nothing seemed to spook him. This behavior is unusual for dogs shortly after they become lost. Every caller said basically the same thing. "He didn't act frightened or nervous." One of the volunteers, Joan Schilling, had agreed to have her phone number on the signs and was kept busy checking out the areas where he was being reported. Finally, she caught sight of him.

"He looked at me as if to say, 'I know you're looking for me, but I'm busy.' If I walked faster, he started to trot away from me. I couldn't believe it when I saw him stop and look both ways before he crossed each street." At that point, he went south again, and she lost him.

Her next phone call was from someone in the Green Bay suburb of Allouez, which was even farther south from where Chester had started out. And then silence. There were no phone calls for three days. Then remarkably, Joan started getting calls from the same route he had taken south. Now, however, he was moving north. He was going back toward the mill. What a relief! That's when we realized that he was still looking for the truck.

The calls indicated that he traveled back the same distance as the mill, but he was a few blocks east of, yet parallel to the route he had taken south. He ended up in an area without homes where there was brush for coverage. Ironically, the Humane Society was close by.

For two days sightings of Chester came from that area. Joan decided to put out dog food. Luckily, Chester found it. We were almost positive from past experiences and calls that it was Chester people had spotted. We hoped the dog food would keep him in the area long enough for us to get him.

Joan had been in constant contact with James, the truck driver. He was now back in Indiana. When she called him with an update, Chester had been returning regularly to the same spot where the dog food was being put out. James and his wife decided to drive all the way from Indiana, hoping to get Chester. We were thrilled, of course, but nervous that Chester might take off before they arrived; or worse, what if it wasn't the right dog? We didn't have a photo; and many times, people don't describe their dogs accurately.

James and his wife left Indiana early that same night. At five o'clock the next morning, Joan's phone rang.

"We've got him!"

Nobody, including the owners, could have been more excited than Joan. "I threw on some clothes," she said, "and probably broke the speed limit to get there. I wanted to know if it was the same dog that I had seen." Thankfully, it was. What a relief. It was the sixteenth day of tracking him. The owners had walked around the area only an hour before Chester had come up behind them.

"Chester was sacked out in the back seat of their car and barely lifted his head for me," Joan said. "I checked his paws. It was amazing. They looked good compared to most dogs having been gone that long. Chester was none the worse for wear, and we were three very happy people."

We all agreed with Joan when she said, "That's one man who really loves his dog."

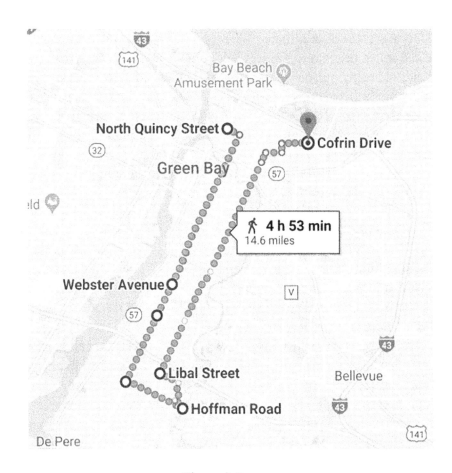

Chester's Journey

Ms

"It's Ms! I know it is! I can't believe it," I said it out loud even though I was alone in the car. It was October, and Ms had been missing since early August.

Rather than get out of the car, I decided to follow her. I drove slowly and as quietly as I could down a bumpy farm road between a tree line and a field of corn, following her at a distance, praying she didn't spook. She kept walking slowly and steadily, veering off to the left and into the cornfield. I couldn't see her anymore.

She was like a precious little windup toy with four dainty feet peeking out of all that fur, just tiptoeing along! Not a clue in that darling little head that there was a family frantically looking for her. If she had only known! I didn't call her, knowing with certainty she would not come, more than likely not even to her owner at this point. Years of tracking Shelties gave me complete confidence in that thought. I stopped at the end of the road and got out of the car as quietly as I could and canvassed a small portion of the cornfield. I didn't know corn was so tall, or was I getting shorter? I did know for sure that the rows were planted closer together than when I was little, because my sister, Bobbie, and I used to be able to run through the cornfields when we played at farms on the outskirts of a little town called Alma Center.

I quietly got back into the car and headed back home thinking about all the lost Shelties I had searched for. A young and healthy dog like Ms was not the typical lost dog I normally pursued, but because she was a Sheltie, I was hooked. It would be one more difficult Sheltie search, but the challenge grabbed at me. It was like a game. A championship game. Who would win—the Sheltie or me?

The chances were almost certain the owner wouldn't find her without our help. Was I overconfident? Maybe, but success breeds confidence, and we certainly had had success. After a week or two of searching, most owners thought that either their dogs were dead, or somebody else had them and wasn't giving them back. Wrong!

To this very day, the word *Sheltie* coupled with *lost* makes me catch my breath. I have never owned one but can say positively it is an awesome dog when it's lost because of its ability to survive. At one time I could count twelve Shelties that we had helped owners look for. We had found all but one. Story after story, each rescue was remarkable. The Shelties would be missing for weeks, months, and two of them had survived a Wisconsin winter! If the ability to survive on its own is an indication of a dog's intelligence, then anyone who has tracked a lost Sheltie would put it at the top of the list.

Once a Sheltie is lost, it is the most elusive of dogs. While frustrating for the owners, it is good for the Sheltie because it is able to avoid predators such as coyotes.

Most of the Shelties our group has tracked have stayed within a two-mile radius of where they ended up on the first day they were lost. Unfortunately, it's not possible to say where it will end up on that first day.

Many Sheltie owners are not aware of the elusive side of their dog's personality. After seeing the same scenario so many times, I almost felt obligated to alert owners to this phenomenon. Because owners' perceptions regarding the whereabouts of their dogs were often wrong, I would frequently hint that their dogs were safe but most likely hunkered down someplace. The majority of people with lost Shelties never believed it was possible to lose their dogs. Often, these owners said they never let their dogs off leash, or "No, she's always right next to me," or "She never leaves our yard." This puzzled me. Rather than making them defensive, I often dropped the subject.

Arriving back home, I sat in the car thinking back to the day I got the call that Ms was missing. She belonged to Linda, and it was obvious they were buddies. When Linda traveled, she often took Ms with her and never once worried about her taking off.

Linda's description of Ms (pronounced *Miz*) was touching. "She's adorable. Being only twenty-one pounds, she was just like a little toy Lassie, except that she was mostly black with some white and a little brown. I named her Ms because, just like her name implies, she's as feisty as any advocate for women's rights. She's especially cute when she stomps her front feet and swings her head back and forth while looking up to you as if to say, 'Let's go, let's go!'"

It had been a nice summer's day, the first week of August, and Ms was temporarily staying with the owner's daughter on the outskirts of a little town called De Pere. The daughter and her friend Jeff were playing with Ms in the backyard when suddenly, there was a loud bang, like a car backfiring.

"We looked around, and Ms was gone. Just like that!" I had heard that story before. In fact, too many times. Sudden voices, strange noises were often the culprit for a lost dog, especially if it was in a strange place; and besides that—a Sheltie—a double whammy!

Throughout the United States, not all lost dogs are brought to a local shelter or posted *lost/found* in the media. People don't know what to do when a dog is lost. They don't always know what to do to recover their pets. If the owner hasn't found his or her dog within two or three days, then signs are the most important tool. Because of our success finding lost dogs using signs, we learned to fine-tune them and knew that signs were a must-do. We learned this because we had questioned people who had responded to our signs, so we became aware of what wording was important. There was no question about it. Most importantly, the driver of a car must be able to read a sign when driving by at the speed limit. Knowing this should be stressed, we always said, "Remember, the person driving the car is not going to stop, get out of the car, go over and read the sign, and go back to his or her car." Because of our experience and success, owners of lost pets were grateful that we would make the signs. They would pick them up, and we would give ideas of where to post them.

When you are making signs, certain breeds have to be identified differently. Samoyeds, for example, should be called *large, white, fluffy dog*. Few people know what a Samoyed is. The majority of people know that there is no such thing as a toy collie, but they get the idea quickly when that wording is used. Strangely, many people think a Sheltie is an English sheepdog. The signs for Shelties usually looked like this:

$100 REWARD
TOY COLLIE
920-336-XXXX

Another issue when making signs is the mistaken idea that a driver can read a computer-generated sign. The print is too small and doesn't stand out to catch someone's attention.

Lost-dog signs went up for Ms the very day we got the call she went missing. Linda, my friend Cathy Donlevy, and I put up the signs as quickly as we could. Linda had already put an ad in the local newspaper and on the radio, but this was the third day, and Linda had not gotten one call.

After the signs went up, I began thinking about all the different people who might be able to help us locate Ms. Early on in my adventures with the lost dogs, I had discovered a great ally in Ed Kazik, the superintendent of the county highway department patrol. Dogs from the city often ended up on the edge of town or in the country or in industrial parks. Perhaps, because it was quieter than in town, yet there were people close by. Dogs were easier to spot in those areas, and that's the area that Ed and his men drove regularly. If a dog was hit and killed by a car, Ed and his crew would be in charge of removing it. Cars are the biggest enemy of lost dogs in a country setting, but amazingly, not with a Sheltie. I have never known one to be hit by a car, although surely some are. If Ed and his men weren't already experts on descriptions and breeds, they became experts fast.

Hunters and farmers were another great source of help with lost dogs in the country. Many times, hunters brought lost dogs right to their homes if they were tagged. Keisha was one of these lucky ones. A totally blind keeshond, she slipped her electronic collar on the first day of deer hunting. Because she was almost the size of a small deer, her owners were frantic. Fortunately, within one hour of her signs going up, some hunters called the Falcks—Keisha's owners—and directed them right to their dog.

Any time a dog in the country went missing, I automatically made a call to Ed. I did so for Ms in early August, when she was first reported lost; but when Ed called me late in September and said, "Hey, did you ever find that Sheltie you were looking for in the De Pere area?" I had to stop and think for a minute. That was two months ago, and I had probably been involved with at least sixteen to twenty different lost dogs in that time period. He continued, "I saw a little Sheltie by John VanDuerzan's farm over on Highway G." After he reminded me where Highway G was, I thought of Ms right away. It definitely could be her. But could it really be? She had been missing for almost two months.

I raced to finish my real estate schedule for the day and drove out to John's farm. On the way out, the thought, *wouldn't it be nice if I got paid for finding lost dogs?* crossed my mind, knowing full well I would do it regardless. The success stories kept me going from one dog to the next.

As I pulled up to the house, John came over to the car to greet me. He was pleasant and easy to talk to, so I knew right away that this was the perfect place for Ms to hide out. She had been gone for over two months. What took her so long to find this location? Where had she been? John had seen her that day and could describe her to a T. The rest of John's family had seen her throughout the week, but nobody could get near her.

Linda arrived shortly after I did. John described Ms exactly, even to the little bit of brown. Their farm was a long way from where Ms had taken off, but we felt from John's description that it was definitely her. John and his wife, Barb, had heard their dogs barking several times at night. Now they wondered whether it's because Ms was scavenging for some leftover dog food. We pushed all doubt aside. The hunt was on. Ms was alive!

Driving out of the driveway to go home, I realized what a perfect hideout this was for Ms. It had a shallow stream for water nearby, a small patch of woods, all the corn she would need for cover, and a quiet little farmhouse nearby. How sad that it took her two months.

Again I wondered, *where had she been all this time?* Had she been here hiding and just started coming out in the daytime when someone could see her?

That night, Linda and I put out dog food. Hopefully, Ms would see or smell it. Linda drove slowly while I sprinkled it along the road, but not so far out on the road, she might be hit by a car if she was eating it. She might be so starved at this point that she wouldn't notice a car coming, yet we wanted to remain optimistic that Ms might find the food!

Late the next day, we noticed Barb picking up some of the dog food that we had put out. She thought it was too close to their house. She had observed her own dogs crossing the road to get at it, and she was afraid they might get hit by a car. A new lesson learned! A common sense one at that!

Judy Fuller, the owner of the first lost dog I had helped, and I discussed trapping Ms. Now, many years later, Judy was a dog constable for her area and had successfully trapped many dogs. She and her husband, George, had become what I considered experts; and I valued their opinions.

Judy told me, "You will have to stop putting out dog food except for the trap, or you will never make it necessary for her to go into the trap." That thought was scary to me because we had seen Ms from a distance, and she was eating some of the food on the road. I was terrified she wouldn't go in the trap. Having seen her only from a distance, we couldn't tell how thin she was under her full coat. With the help of the crows, most of the food was gone now.

I finally relented, conceding, "We just have to risk it."

We started that night with some fishy-smelling cat food. Success! Except, it wasn't Ms. It was a cat. Three different barn cats. One each day, for three days in a row! They were easy to release, happy to get away, and never trapped again.

But then it happened! Our biggest fear! A skunk! Luckily, Jeff, Linda's daughter's boyfriend, became an expert at getting the skunk out with a series of large wooden stakes. He found it best if he let the skunk simmer down by throwing a towel over the trap and letting it sit for a few hours. Fortunately, the temperature was just right for that approach. If the temperature were too hot or cold outside, the skunk's survival would become an issue. I was impressed that as an amateur, Jeff never once got sprayed.

Trapping Ms was beginning to look futile. Would it help if Ms could see Linda in a quiet setting at night? Willing at that point to try anything, we had Linda sit out in a cornfield where Ms had often appeared. She could be reading a book with a flashlight, as it would be dark out. A weird idea. We were desperate. I sat in my car close to the house, watching for Linda to give me a, "come pick me up," signal with the flashlight. Though we didn't have any sighting of Ms, we did get chilled to the bone. Ms was probably curled up sleeping someplace warm by that time. I felt a little sheepish driving home because it felt like a silly thing to do at night, but a grateful Linda was a good sport about it.

Thoughts of the upcoming cold season were beginning to gnaw at me. I couldn't bear the thought of Ms still being out there. She had food, but we didn't know what shape she was in. As it got colder, I could foresee thinking about her every night, lying in bed gritting my teeth, shutting my eyes tight, and clenching my fists, trying to go to sleep. How do people survive a missing child?

Friends Sue Engberg and Amy Ward spent hours and hours canvassing the cornfields. Not one sighting of Ms. I couldn't do this alone. What would I do without animal-loving friends?

Mulling over what could be done next, I thought of Ms's routine. There was a small patch of woods that seemed to be her home base. What if we used orange plastic fencing that construction people used? We could fence the back of the woods, leaving open the area that she went into and out of. Once she returned at night, we would close the opening she came through, hoping she wouldn't spot us and dart back out. It was worth a try.

We just needed fencing. Hoping to borrow some, I headed out the next morning and stopped at three different construction companies. At the first stop, a pleasant lady checked with someone in the back office who said that theirs was in use; but one big job would be finished this week, so we should check back next week.

At the next construction stop, I approached *Mr. Crabby* who practically growled at me and acted as if he didn't know what a dog was. On to the next construction company.

Discouraged by that afternoon, I approached the Czech Company with apprehension. Mike Kragewski was in the office and came over to the counter when he heard me talking to one of the office girls. It was obvious that he was interested in helping get the dog in any way he could. A dog lover probably, but more important than that, a really nice man. Unlike the case with *Mr. Crabby*, this is usually the case when you ask for someone's help. Mike said that we could use whatever he had in stock that wasn't being used and added, "I'll order some more today. We can always use it. I'll have it in two days." We scheduled the ambush project for the coming weekend.

Now that we knew where Ms was hiding, Jeff spent hours walking the field looking for her, hoping to catch her sleeping so he could just grab her. The day before the fencing project was to begin was no exception.

That day at my office was brutal. A basement inspection had failed. A couple getting a divorce and selling the house changed their minds about signing a good offer. I was tired, crabby, and hungry. How could two nice people be so difficult?

I decided to forget about business and go to my favorite place for lunch. The staff at Mandarin Garden would change my mood. I sat down to a cup of my favorite wonton soup. After the first spoonful, my cellphone rang. I thought to myself, "Geez, why in the heck didn't I turn it off? Why do I let a phone control my life?"

Answering the phone, I said, "Hello," as cheerfully as I could manage.

The voice on the other end of the phone shouted, "We've got her!" Then silence. I changed my focus and tried to think. The voice said, "Bette?"

I responded, "Yes."

"It's Linda! Jeff caught Ms!"

I practically slid to the floor and shut my eyes, thinking, "Thank God."

Grateful that Ms was finally caught, I reflected on a comment that my friend Dorothy always said to me. "You've got an angel sitting on your shoulder."

I thought to myself, "Yes I do, and please, please, please don't fly away!"

Once back home, Ms acted as if she had never left; but shockingly, she had gone from her normal twenty pounds to a skeletal ten and a half pounds, with heavy calluses on her feet. As a result of her unfortunate experience, she developed skin problems that plagued her for the rest of her life.

But she was home. Home at last.

Sheltie comes home

An Allouez woman's two-month search has a joyous ending

Dog home: Lost for two months, Ms. is back with her owner, Linda Schwallie of Allouez. The sheltie was found by Jeff Casperson, left, the boyfriend of Julie Gaston, right, who is Schwallie's daughter.

Press-Gazette photo by John Rubb

By Sean Schultz
Press-Gazette

A missing sheltie and a determined rescue crew resulted in a joyful reunion after more than two months for Ms. and her owner, Linda Schwallie of Allouez.

Ms., a 3-year-old, 18-pound sheltie, was staying at the home of Schwallie's daughter, Julie Gaston, on Grant Street in De Pere when she was spooked and bolted from the yard Aug. 6.

Animal welfare officials were notified, but after three or four weeks, Schwallie "had pretty much given up hope." She feared Ms. was either dead or stolen.

John and Barb Van Deurzen gave her some hope after they spotted a tri-colored sheltie at their farm on Fernando Road in west De Pere on Sept. 21.

Animal welfare volunteer Bette Anderson also spotted a sheltie near the farm.

Pet rescuers sprinkled food in the area and on Sept. 29, Judy Fuller, an animal control agent from Little Suamico, set up a live trap. Anderson said the trap netted two skunks and three cats, but Ms. was too smart for it.

Volunteers, including Amy Ward and Sue Engberg from Amy's Friends Pet Sitting Service, and Schwallie family members continued to comb the area.

Schwallie's daughter and her friend, Jeff Casperson of De Pere, tried one last time to catch Ms. They found her asleep Tuesday, but she bolted again. This time, Casperson caught her.

The delighted couple took Ms. home and waited for an unsuspecting Schwallie to arrive. The reunion was tearful and joyous.

"I just fell apart, I was so excited," Schwallie said.

That night, Ms. was her old self again, but weighed a scant 10 pounds.

"After working for 13 years with lost dogs and cats, I have tremendous respect for the sheltie's sense of survival," Anderson said. "If survival in the wild is any indication of intelligence, then the sheltie is near the top in this dog world."

■ If you lose a pet, report it to the Bay Area Humane Society and Animal Shelter at 435-6150.

Ms and owner Linda

Ms and owner Linda

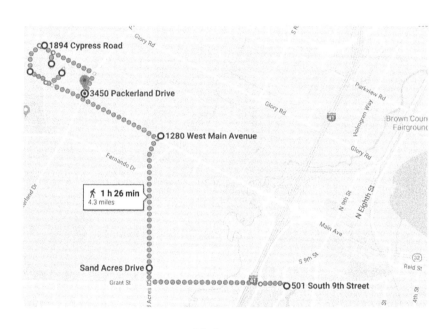

Ms Journey

Ginger

Tracks! I could see them from my car. My heart raced. Could we be this lucky so soon? Nah! I bet they were coyote or fox tracks. Getting out of my car, I saw that they were running in a straight line and parallel to the road. I had never seen that track pattern from a wild animal before. Wild animals usually leave tracks that cross and don't run in a straight line. Actually, looking at them closer, I could see that there was more than one set of tracks; and they were going both ways. I followed the tracks for about two hundred feet or so and then went back to my car. Doubts crept into my mind again. Would a blind dog walk in such a straight line? The tracks were all the same distance from the road, and they were only a half mile from the house where Ginger was lost.

Ginger, blind and deaf, was the devoted companion of an elderly lady by the name of Ethel, who lived in Green Bay. Ethel had taken the dog to visit her friends in the country many times. She always let Ginger wander loose outside. Being part beagle and part dachshund, Ginger naturally loved sniffing around the trees and shrubs and scaring up squirrels and rabbits.

I'd heard these words umpteen times. "She's run around this yard every time I've been out here yet never taken off before."

But in Ginger's case, there was plenty to worry about, so it was tempting to reply, "But she's old and blind now. Things change as they do with us old people."

Except for the cold, there was a huge advantage in looking for dogs during winter in Wisconsin, especially after a fresh snowfall. Dog tracks are hard to miss. I turned right at the next road about a half-mile down, pulled over, and got out of the car. Again, no tracks.

I got back in the car and drove to where I had turned the corner, continuing on straight instead of turning right. Still no tracks. Of course, Ginger could have walked on the road, either straight ahead of me or turned the corner; and the snowplow could have covered her tracks.

Judy, my friend who had helped me so many times with my Lost Dog Project, had also been searching. The only tracks she found were very close to the house. The whole area was mostly plowed fields, which were large chunks of soil. It was a tough area to walk on, jarring one's body with every step. Scanning the area was difficult also: black ground, white snow, black ground. Most dogs would not be out in the middle of the field, but with a blind dog, anything could happen.

By the end of the third day, we were exhausted from searching. We had meticulously searched around the house for at least two miles. Our next point of interest was a patch of woods that covered three or four acres located not too far from the house.

Judy and I discussed our plans for the next morning. They included bringing rolls of toilet paper to mark where each of us had started walking a row. It was a system that had worked well when we were searching for a different dog in rows of corn last fall. With a limited amount of snow now, the woods would be like rutted fields, hard to walk on. Alternating areas of ground cover, snow, trees, and brush, I consoled myself that it would be easier walking than if there had been two feet of snow. Judy's son, Rick, didn't have school the next day, so he would join us and be an extra set of eyes.

Judy and Rick decided to drive the roads again, searching for Ginger until I arrived. Rick carried binoculars. Judy drove past the area where I had first spotted the dog tracks. She swung the car around to the right and had gone less than a quarter of a mile.

"Stop! A dog," Rick yelled. Judy slammed on the brakes. Rick got excited as he told the story of finding Ginger. "I tore out of the car," he said, "and ran as fast as I could. Each step jarred my body as I hit row after row of that frozen dirt. I was so afraid she would run. I knew that she couldn't because of her age and condition, but I wasn't thinking rationally at that point. If she hadn't picked up her head the minute she did, I wouldn't have seen her, and more than likely, she would have died there."

"I scooped her up and put her under my jacket," Rick continued. "She was shivering so hard it felt like something was banging against my chest. It took almost an hour to get here, and she was still shaking with cold when I put her down on the table. Now I understand why it's such a big deal when my mom finds a lost dog."

In spite of Ginger's fragile condition and being so cold, she would soon be going home.

Ginger

Ginger's owner, Ethel Stencil, and members of her family

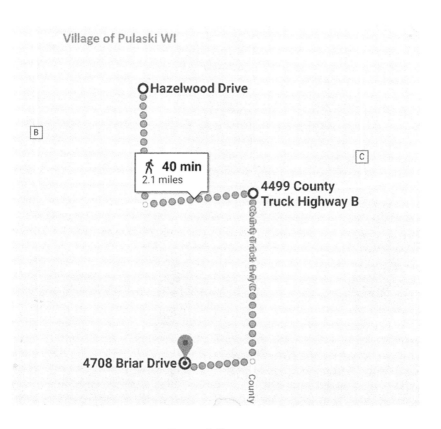

Ginger's Journey

Cujo

C ujo was the dog I remembered after my first visit with Leon. Cujo quickly got my attention. He had a strange intensity about him, almost eerie. His gray and black fur seemed unusual; and at times, his large ears stood up at strange angles. My first thought was that he was a wolf or a wolf hybrid. Had Leon not been a quiet and obviously gentle man, I might have been spooked. I didn't want to seem intrusive, so I didn't say anything or ask any questions about Cujo that day.

Leon's friendship was just one of the many that those of us active with the volunteer Keshena Animal Help and Rescue Group had formed. Almost fifty years of animal-welfare work preceded my goal of organizing the group of volunteers to improve the lives of the cats and dogs on the Menominee Indian Reservation in northeastern Wisconsin. In the process of bringing their rampant heartworm problem under control, spaying and neutering hundreds of dogs and cats, and subsidizing emergency veterinarian costs, we came to know many of the Native Americans personally. It was easy to become attached to many of their pets and just as easy to become attached to many of the people. One of those friendships was with a man named Leon Cardish.

That day, I was at Leon's house to check on how his dog Missy was doing. Leon had not requested our help; but previously, when a volunteer had delivered heartworm preventive pills, she had discovered the dog had suffered a serious injury in the woods. A sharp stick had punctured her skin in the chest area, and Leon had been trying to doctor Missy himself. The wound area looked clean, but it was quite red around the injury, and there were several areas with oozing pus. It didn't look good. I had made arrangements for a veterinary visit; and after that first visit, I stopped by regularly to see how the wound was healing.

Leon had two dogs, Cujo and Missy. They were polar opposites. Missy looked and acted like the typical Labrador and golden retriever mix—gentle, loving, and outgoing, the type of dog who would plunk right down at the feet of a stranger to have her tummy rubbed. In contrast, Cujo stood back and watched, looking as if he'd jump in any minute if anything or anyone were to threaten Missy.

There was also a scattering of cats in the home, one a very striking gray and white cat named Scampy. Scampy let me know he was there by continuously wagging his tail, kind of like poking a finger in my face. They were part of the family.

Eventually, Leon told me the fascinating story of Cujo.

"A few years ago," he began, "we had what I remember as a really long winter. One spring morning, I let Missy out, and she charged down the steps and headed for something gray. As she turned, I could see that it was a puppy. Shaggy with big ears, the puppy stood very still. Missy sniffed it. I wondered what she would do. I wasn't worried that she would hurt it because people had dropped off dogs before, and she had never hurt or bothered any of them."

"I walked toward the puppy, but it started running for the woods, so I stopped and went back and stood on the porch. I wondered why a puppy that small would run away. Missy started walking back to the porch and then lay down about halfway back. The puppy turned around and came back too. Then Scampy, the cat, came out but stiffened as soon as he saw the puppy. The puppy looked at the cat but didn't move. I thought that was a little strange because in my experience, most puppies wanted to play with cats or kittens, and the young cats or kittens accepted that unless the puppy would play too rough."

He went on with his story. I listened intently. "I thought at first, the puppy looked like a wolf puppy and that more than likely its mother would come looking for it that same night. We have wolves here on the reservation, so I wasn't surprised to see it, but when I went to let Missy out the following morning, I couldn't believe it. He was still here."

Leon stopped his story for a moment, and I thought to myself, *I'm glad I'm not the only one who thinks that Cujo is most likely a wolf.* I could see that Leon was very attached to him just by the way he smiled when he looked at him. He surely would not want to give him up if there were restrictions about keeping a wolf on the reservation. I never did check on the restrictions. Leon went on with his story."

"Once I let Missy out again," he continued, "the puppy ran to her. Missy just followed her normal routine of checking out the yard and eventually peed in her regular spot. The puppy followed suit. In fact, he did everything Missy did except eat. I put out a separate dish for Cujo and kept Missy away from it, but he still didn't eat. A few days passed before he finally started to pick at the food."

"Every time I came out in the morning, I noticed the puppy coming out from under the porch. The porch is enclosed on three sides, and that's where he slept for almost a year."

"I started calling him Cujo, and he reacted to the name right away, but he still wouldn't come to me. It was almost a year before he came to me when I called his name. His normal routine was to follow and stay close to Missy. When spring came, he finally followed Missy into the house."

"Cujo hated the hot weather and panted really hard, but I didn't spray him with water like I did Missy because I thought it would scare him. Cujo was very interested when I cooked, but he never begged for food. When Missy barked, Cujo howled, especially if I had company," Leon said.

My thoughts interrupted his story as I remembered hearing Cujo howl. It reminded me of a howling sound I had heard as a child, coming from the woods in back of my grandpa's house up north. I had heard Cujo howl more than once, and it was a memorable experience. It was so wolflike. It was eerie. In my mind, I can hear it yet.

Leon continued his story. "Cujo eventually got up on the sofa and lay next to Missy. He never had to be housebroken. He just followed Missy outside. He wouldn't let me put a collar on him and uttered a low growl if I tried."

Years passed, and I continued to visit Leon and his family of pets. Cujo never got really big, probably no more than sixty pounds. On one of those visits, I noticed Cujo had an ugly red patch on his flank. I suspected that it might be mange, a serious, destructive skin problem caused by mites, and often seen on foxes and wolves in the wild. Dr. Steve De Grave was in town for the free clinic and agreed to come over and look at Cujo. It was impossible for a stranger to get close to Cujo, so Dr. Steve was not able to get a skin scraping; but seeing him from a distance, he was certain that it was mange.

There are two types of mange, sarcoptic and demodectic. One is usually treatable by dipping the dog in a solution, but that was not an option. Leon had an arm injury on one side and a hand injury on the other side. The drug Ivomec would treat either type of mange; but not having had any experience treating wolves with Ivomec, Dr. Steve had Leon start with a very low dosage of it on Cujo's food. He gradually increased the dosage.

I made extra trips to check on Cujo. The treatment was going well. The affected skin area was starting to look better. We were fortunate that Cujo had not noticed the medicine in his food.

Just as the skin condition started to heal, my hopes came to a screeching halt. I noticed a fiery-red tumor by Cujo's mouth. I had an ominous feeling. We needed to get Cujo to Dr. Steve's clinic in Green Bay. Cujo had never been in a car before. In fact, Leon had told me that while Cujo would do almost anything Missy did, the one thing Cujo wouldn't do was follow her into a car. Therefore, transporting Cujo would be difficult. I tried to put a collar on Cujo at that point. He wagged his tail, looked right at me, and uttered a quiet but distinct growl. I dropped the collar. Cujo was still in charge. At that point, Dr. Steve and I decided to test Cujo on tranquilizers. That way, Cujo could be transported to the clinic safely. It took almost three weeks of experimenting with the tranquilizer before we could determine a sufficient yet safe amount.

Once a proper tranquilizer dosage was determined, Leon and Jason, another volunteer got Cujo into a crate. I drove as Jason kept an eye on Cujo. Leon decided to stay home. The fifty-mile trip to the clinic went well, but that is all that went well. Dr. Steve's diagnosis was heartbreaking. He discovered that Cujo had an advanced case of a devastating form of cancer called hemangiosarcoma. We could easily see the big tumor, but we hadn't noticed the other small tumors that had formed on his body. Dr. Steve had. We all realized then that it was time for Cujo to leave us. It was a very emotional situation; but after my conversation on the phone with Leon, it became evident that he made the right decision.

It was a quiet, sad trip home for Jason and me. Friendships like the one between Leon and Cujo are few and far between. They were blessed to have each other. The volunteers, who had worked with Cujo over the years—Gaynelle, Lisa, and me—were honored to have known them both. Two creatures who did the best they could with what they were given.

We still see Leon, Missy, and Scamper regularly. We also have made friends with Bella, a little tyke of a dog who is now Missy's constant companion.

Bella's a feisty little black and tan terrier and dances around as all terriers do, making it her unrequested business to protect everyone and everything including the cats. Even though Missy appears content, Bella will never be another Cujo. Could any dog be?

Missy, Cujo and Scampy

Leon

Missy and Scampy

Reflections

The Lost Dog Project was a time of incredible highs. Mostly from the interaction with lost pet owners. The desperation in their hearts couldn't be hidden from their faces, neither could the expression of relief when we found their pets. Regardless of the outcome, owners often showed gratitude for our work by sending photos of their pets, mementos, poems, and other items of thanks. Though we always started out as strangers, bonding with the owners was inevitable as we worked to accomplish the goal—to change the look of desperation to one of relief.

Passing years and age have erased some of the names of the dogs and cats rescued, but the images of their situations remain vividly in my mind.

The Lost Dog Project received a number of significant awards, but those could not compare to the heartfelt thanks of the dog and cat owners. Those thanks wouldn't have been possible without the people involved in the project—the shelter staff who called us with the lost reports, the volunteers who acted as intermediaries with the desperate owners to absorb their heart-wrenching phone calls.

There were many other individuals who provided critical information and help—the holding facilities, the county highway workers, farmers, hunters, mail carriers, and bus drivers. I was especially grateful to the volunteers who helped make and put up the lost-pet signs, spent endless hours searching in the snow, the cold, the heat, and the rain for the lost pets, and never complained about being late for family get-togethers, social events, and appointments.

We were an incredibly successful team—one that lived by the saying, "It's only with the heart one can see rightly, what's essential is invisible to the eye."

Finding Lost Dogs and Cats

To most people, losing a pet can be like losing a member of the family. After twenty years of volunteering in animal welfare work, I spent the next twenty-five years helping people find their lost pets, a lot of them elderly pets. There were many other dedicated volunteers who helped with this project; and together, we tried various strategies. Some of them worked, and some didn't. After several years, we felt we had perfected our strategies and were encouraged by our success. We were amazed at the amount of people who were interested in what we were doing. People we had never met, and people who had never seen the missing pets. I realized very quickly that owners of lost pets were completely unaware of two very important facts:

1. There are many places to call or check when looking for a lost pet, not just your local humane society or shelter.
2. Both cats and dogs can survive on their own much longer than the average person thinks, regardless of the weather or the pet's age.

Why Pets Become Lost

After looking at literally thousands of cards describing missing dogs and cats at the local humane society, I've seen enough evidence to conclude that, other than carelessness, the majority of pets are lost for one of four reasons:

1. "They are old and become disoriented—just like people." (A statement made by my veterinary friend and mentor, Dr. Sam Vainisi, the impetus that started me on this Lost Dog Project.)
2. Someone other than the pet's owner is taking care of the pet (either at its home or the caretaker's home), or the pet is in a new home.
3. Inexperienced dog owners are unaware that young and unneutered male dogs are able to smell a female in heat miles away and will often run in search of that smell but are then unable to find their way home.
4. Dog owners are unaware that loud noises (fireworks, thunderstorms, and gunshots) can cause dogs to be frightened. They frequently try to run away from these very predictable situations; and if not properly confined or restrained, they can become lost.

Steps Most Owners Take to Find Their Missing Pets

1. Search the area where the pet disappeared, both by foot and car
2. Call the local humane society and police department
3. Place an ad in the local newspaper, and call the radio stations (in smaller towns)
4. Make an announcement on social media
5. Monitor the internet

These common steps are all good and necessary, but most people fail to do the remaining steps listed below. These remaining steps are critical. They can make the difference in whether a lost pet is recovered.

6. Check all holding facilities. Call the police and the sheriff's departments and ask who is responsible for picking up stray animals in the area in which your pet was lost. If you live in or near rural areas, it may be the town chairman or constable. Every area will have someone assigned to pick up strays, though it may not be the same person during the day as it is at night. If the person responsible is not a shelter employee, he or she may do one of several things. The person may hold the animal at the office, government facility, or his or her home and turn it into the shelter later; or the animal could be transported to the shelter immediately.

More alarming, *the person may be able to legally keep the dog for a specific length of time and then sell it or dispose of it.*

Our strategy was to call the person who was responsible for picking up strays in the immediate vicinity. In addition, we'd call people responsible for picking up strays in all vicinities surrounding that primary area. We would inform them of the lost pet. This often involved five or six different people. Either the pet owner or one of our volunteers would keep a list of these phone numbers and call for updates every two or three days. This would go on for weeks or until the lost pet was found.

7. Check surrounding counties. There are times when drivers pick up dogs running on a highway and don't know where to take them until they get home. Once home, they take the dogs to their local shelters and tell staff where they picked them up. They may also contact shelters in the area where they found the dogs. Several things may go wrong from this point on. For instance, the owner may not have called the shelter to report the missing dog yet; and when the owner does, the shelter may fill out a missing dog report but may not check this lost dog against the *found dog* file to cross-reference data. And then there is the possibility that a found card may not even have been filled out.

    Another scenario is that stray dogs may not always go to the shelter. In outlying areas, stray dogs may go to someone assigned the responsibility of caring for them. In Wisconsin, that person could be a constable, who may not be responsible for taking dogs to the shelter. Constables may just keep them, find another home for them, or have them put down. The responsibility of having a dog properly identified is always the owner's. Tags or microchips or both belong on every pet.

8. Go to the local humane society immediately rather than calling. An owner's description of a lost pet and a shelter employee's description of a pet that has been turned in often differ. It's best to go to the shelter in person to avoid

this confusion. File a report while there. Go every day. Look at all the animals in their possession. Your diligence will help create a special awareness to the shelter employees and help them stay focused on identifying your lost pet if it comes in.

9. In addition to checking all the holding facilities, don't forget to check with the county, city, and village road crews to inquire about whether a dead dog fitting the description has been picked up.

10. Make up good signs. We found that if the pet doesn't show up by the next day at the local shelter, putting up signs is the most important thing to be done. Remember, if people see a stray cat or dog, they will rarely call the animal shelter or check the internet; but they will call a telephone number on a sign. Have everyone in the area help search. They have no reason to look for an animal if they don't know it's missing, and they are not going to check the internet regularly to see what animals are missing. Our rescue efforts found that the most successful signs had these elements in common:

    a. Use heavyweight waterproof white paper, approximately fourteen inches by sixteen inches.

    b. Use four lines or fewer.

    c. The size of the print must be readable by someone driving by at the speed limit. Remember that people do not stop the car, get out, and read the sign. If they have seen the animal, most people will stop to get the phone number.

    d. Print in all capital letters *by hand*. If not printed by hand, it doesn't capture attention. Computer-generated signs are hard to read and look like government notices.

    e. Use wide-tipped waterproof *black* markers because other colors fade quickly. Black is easier to read from a distance.

f. Do not waste space by including a picture. Pictures can't be seen from a distance.

g. The top line should always state, "REWARD." It is rare that finders of lost pets will take a reward. The word *reward* emphasizes that a person is missing his or her lost pet. Knowing someone has offered a reward in hopes of finding a lost pet creates an emotion that causes people to want to become more involved. Some examples of signs are depicted below:

$100 REWARD BLACK LAB 920-000-0000	REWARD OLD BROWN DOG LARGE 920-000-0000	REWARD TOY COLLIE (SHELTIE) 920-000-0000	$75 REWARD SHEP MIX 920-000-0000	REWARD BLIND LAB BLACK 920-000-0000
REWARD LARGE WHITE FLUFFY DOG 920-000-0000	REWARD WEINER DOG 920-000-0000	REWARD TIGER CAT BLACK- GREYGRAY 920-000-0000	REWARD SMALL BROWN DOG—DEAF 920-000-0000	$100 REWARD SMALL TAN DOG SCARED DON'T CHASE 920-000-0000

11. Placement of signs
    a. Put on telephone poles or stand-alone wire-sign holders (political or real estate sign holders, for example). Do not put on stop signs, as they will be taken down.
    b. Put two nails, three inches apart, on both the top and bottom of the sign. If only one nail is used, the wind from behind will bend the sign in half, and it won't be readable.
    c. Do not wrap signs around poles. They are not as readable or as noticeable.
    d. Place signs so they can be read from a distance. People won't be able to read them up close if they have to swing their heads and read them as they pass by.
    e. When placing a sign at an intersection, place the sign toward traffic that doesn't stop so it can be easily read.
    f. Take the signs down after the animal is found. If you don't, the chances of the next person posting new signs

might be affected. If the signs were up a long time, we put "Found—Thanks" on them for a few days before we took them down. It was amazing how many calls we got thanking us for doing this.

g. If you get a call regarding a sighting, don't remove the sign unless you are certain the right pet has been identified. The call may be a false alarm. If the right pet has been sighted, add more signs in the direction of the call.

12. Post flyers
   a. Passing out flyers works well in country areas.
   b. Tape flyers to glass or metal, not wood or plastic because they don't stick.
   c. Tape to the outside of mailboxes in the country.
   d. Handwritten flyers are more likely to be read than typed flyers.

13. Pay attention to descriptions
   a. Every word on inquiries and signs makes a difference. Many people do not know breeds of dogs and cats. Many cat owners do not know the correct description of their own cats, such as tortoise and dilute tortoise. They often call them calicos.
   b. For signs and flyers, use words that describe the lost pet's colors. For calicos, use *calico cat—black, orange, white spots*; for tortoise, use *black-orange blend* (with white if that is the case); and with dilute tortoise, *use gray-tan blend*, or other appropriate wording.
   c. The words male or female are not necessary on signs or flyers.
   d. If the animal is mostly black, for instance, write the word *black* on sign.
   e. If the cat is Persian or Angora, include words *long hair* or *fluffy*. The same words or *shaggy* can be used for a dog with similar fur.
   f. Do not use types for cats unless they are Siamese or calico, which are the only cats commonly known.

Additional Information

1. Traps
    Our group had the most success using traps in finding lost cats. These work especially well for cats that are strictly house cats hiding in the neighborhood. Typically, these cats won't come to the door because they are usually spooked by other people. They will not stand still to allow someone to catch them. Dogs that are frightened or spooked are very hard to trap. They are often too smart to get caught in a trap. Shelties are one of the hardest to catch. Dog traps are expensive, making them hard to borrow. We usually chained ours so no one would steal them. Putting tuna inside the trap works best for attracting cats, and hot dogs and braunschweiger works best to attract dogs. Liquid smoke on meat (dark-brown bottle found in the barbecue sauce aisle in the grocery store) is effective and keeps its smells in extremely cold weather.

2. Search-and-rescue dogs
    Our group never had the opportunity to use professionally trained search-and-rescue dogs. Many times we used dogs that belonged to people active in our group. They included red setters, springers, and Chesapeakes—all well controlled and trained on birds. We used them when there were large areas of woods or fields with long grasses to cover. They all had successes and indicated their finds by barking or tail-wagging excitement. Toward the end of our project, we used a trained German shepherd tracker. Within a half hour, he followed a trail to the edge of a river with thin ice.

We found the dog's body in the river in that area in the spring.

3. Ponds, rivers, and railroad tracks

They all claim a lot of dogs—especially the ponds and rivers when the ice is thin. If there are railroad tracks nearby, put up a sign that the train engineers can see. They are very good at calling.

4. Frightened and spooked dogs

Many dogs—notably Shelties, collies, and a lot of the smaller breeds—become easily frightened when lost. Their owners are usually amazed that when they finally spot their dogs, the dogs will not recognize them or their voices and will run from them. If you see your dog and it runs from you, kneel down and talk to it in a normal voice, just loud enough for it to hear. Keep quiet. Do not shout. The dog has probably been chased a lot already.

5. Sprinkling dry dog food

If there have been sightings, sprinkling food on the side of the road will, hopefully, keep the dog in the area. Do not put food in piles because the dog may not travel straight along the road. It may crisscross periodically. Therefore, if food is dribbled along the road, there is more chance of the dog smelling it and seeing it. You want the dog to be seen but not hit by a car when eating. Be careful of putting food too close to homes that have dogs, which might entice them to go on the road. This practice is especially successful on country roads and can be done at night and in wintertime, when the food is especially noticeable on the snow. It can be done from the passenger seat of a car with the person not having to get out.

6. Cats and very old dogs

Signs are a priority. They will be seen by a lot more people, but flyers can let people know the animal is lost right in their area. Information can be more personalized on a flyer. Window wells (really important!), under porches, in garages, and around woodpiles are key places to look for cats and old dogs. Owners can be asked to check these places in flyers. Our volunteers check everything except garages. No one has ever made a complaint about volunteers being on private property. Volunteers knocked on doors and asked whether they could check the window wells and under porches. They usually checked if no one was home. People were always exceptionally nice and very often wanted to talk about an animal they had lost.

7. Tags, microchips, and S-hooks

Once you have your dog back, make certain it has a nametag with your current phone number affixed to the collar with a circular key chain hook instead of an S-hook, which comes off too often. Most dogs seem to get lost on the weekend, so the rabies tag number won't help. Dogs with nametags are returned faster than those with microchips. One concern is that people, who are legally assigned to hold stray dogs, such as constables, do not even have a wand to read a microchip. Obviously, it is best to have the identification tag, the microchip, and the rabies tag. The microchip gives legal proof that it is your dog, and the rabies tag gives the name of the vet clinic used in the event your dog has been hurt while it was lost.

About the Author

Bette spent her early childhood days in Western Wisconsin, in a family with four girls. The family moved often as her father, a Depot Agent, transferred from one depot to the next. Even at a young age, people were an interesting study for Bette. She found it exciting and challenging to make new friends, friends that she would keep for the rest of her life. There was only one *glitch* for Bette growing up. At six, she developed diphtheria which temporarily slowed down her playing *cowboys* with her sister Bobbie and the neighborhood boys. It was an advantage for her cat Sandy to lay on her bed and develop her love for animals. The family settled in Green Bay—headquarters for the railroad—where Bette and Emmy, a star quarterback in high school, became sweethearts.

Bette and Emmy married when Emmy came home from the service and made their home in Green Bay. Bette's family remained close even though scattered throughout the country. Bette and Emmy both cherished their nephews and nieces and saw them regularly, especially in the summer at the lake up north. Bette met the challenge of and enjoyed three different careers: a business school instructor, corporate buyer for the H.C. Prange chain of department stores, and eventually, real estate as a partner and sales agent for Mark D. Olejniczak Realty Inc.

Throughout her careers and up until this day, she has spent over sixty years doing what she calls *heavy duty* animal welfare work. This included starting or helping start Humane Society's in Green Bay, Shawano, Sturgeon Bay, Oconto, and on the Menominee Indian Reservation. She served on the first board of directors for each.

Bette has received numerous awards including State of Wisconsin Veterinary Award and the Green Bay Packer Community Quarterback Award for her Lost Dog Project.

The painting of Bette and her pets, Jones, Blondie, Timber, and Crickett was done by Ms. VanLanen in 1998 and is a cherished gift from a grateful lost dog owner.

Printed in the USA
CPSIA information can be obtained
at www.ICGtesting.com
LVHW090053131123
763661LV00070B/2986